DC
COMICS™
SUPER
HEROES™

THE DARK KNIGHT

BATMAN UNDERCOVER

WRITTEN BY
PAUL WEISSBURG

COVER ILLUSTRATED BY
TIM LEVINS

ILLUSTRATED BY
LUCIANO VECCHIO

BATMAN CREATED BY BOB KANE

STONE ARCH BOOKS
a capstone imprint

PUBLISHED BY STONE ARCH BOOKS IN 2013
A CAPSTONE IMPRINT
1710 ROE CREST DRIVE
NORTH MANKATO, MN 56003
WWW.CAPSTONEPUB.COM

CATALOGING-IN-PUBLICATION DATA IS AVAILABLE AT THE
LIBRARY OF CONGRESS WEBSITE.

ISBN: 978-1-4342-4094-1 (LIBRARY BINDING)
ISBN: 978-1-4342-4213-6 (PAPERBACK)

SUMMARY: THE COSMIC ANNIHILATOR, A DOOMSDAY WEAPON
CAPABLE OF DESTROYING ENTIRE PLANETS, HAS GONE
MISSING! BATMAN IS ON THE CASE, BUT SO FAR THE ONLY
CLUE IS A TICKET TO THE SUPER-VILLAIN CRIME CONVENTION.
THAT'S ONE PLACE THE DARK KNIGHT CAN'T GO . . . SO HE
DECIDES TO ATTEND AS THE MOBSTER, MATCHES MALONE,
INSTEAD.

ART DIRECTOR: BOB LENTZ
DESIGNER: BRANN GARVEY

PRINTED IN THE UNITED STATES OF AMERICA IN
STEVENS POINT, WISCONSIN.
082013   007679R

TABLE OF CONTENTS

WHILE STILL A BOY, BRUCE WAYNE WITNESSED THE BRUTAL MURDER OF HIS PARENTS. THE TRAGIC EVENT CHANGED THE YOUNG BILLIONAIRE FOREVER. BRUCE VOWED TO RID GOTHAM CITY OF EVIL AND KEEP ITS PEOPLE SAFE FROM CRIME. AFTER YEARS OF TRAINING HIS BODY AND MIND, HE DONNED A NEW UNIFORM AND A NEW IDENTITY.

HE BECAME...

THE
DARK KNIGHT™

CHAPTER 1

MATCHES MALONE

On a Gotham City subway train, Matches Malone fidgeted restlessly. Malone was a two-bit criminal on his way to make the biggest deal of his life. He wore a green plaid suit and tinted glasses, but his behavior was even stranger than his clothing. Every few minutes he'd try to engage a fellow subway passenger in extremely annoying small talk.

"So," he said to a middle-aged woman in a business suit. "Come here often?"

The woman sneered at Malone. "Every work day," she snarled. "Leave me alone, you creep!"

Matches shrugged. He went and sat next to an elderly man with a long, gray beard. "How's it going, Grandpa?" Matches said. "Liking the weather?"

"The . . . weather?" the old man said. "We're in a subway, you dolt! And it's raining cats and dogs outside. Get away from me."

Malone shrugged and moved on down the subway car. He started to sit down next to a young woman, but she blocked the seat with her hands.

"*HISSSSSSSSSSSS!*" she snarled at him.

Matches jumped back. "Yikes!" he cried out.

Matches gave up hope of finding casual conversation and found a seat in the back of the subway car as the train rose above ground. Matches loved talking with folks, but most of the time they didn't enjoy talking with him. That made him angry.

RRRRRRRING! The criminal's cell interrupted his brooding. He flicked open the phone and listened. "I'll be there in a few minutes," he said. "You just make sure you don't forget to bring the money!"

The old man nearby wrapped himself in his blankets and glared at Matches. In front of the old man stood a shopping cart stuffed with plastic bags, empty bottles, and old newspapers.

Just some homeless guy, Matches thought.

When the subway stopped at the station closest to Harper Pier, Matches Malone stepped outside, still shouting into his cell phone. "Look, buddy," he said, "if you want this thing, you better come out to the pier right now. I'm not going to sit around and wait all night!"

Just before the subway doors closed, the old man got up and jumped out of the car, leaving behind his shopping cart. The old man moved with surprising quickness. He was graceful and agile, like a trained athlete. That's because the old man wasn't an old man at all . . .

He was Batman!

The Dark Knight had been following Matches Malone in disguise all night. And now he was about to catch his prey.

As Batman trailed Matches out of the subway station, Batman spoke softly into the earpiece that was hidden by his fake beard. "Robin," he said, "Matches is headed toward Harper Pier."

Several miles away, the Boy Wonder started his motorcycle and raced toward the pier. This was a very important case. Matches Malone had gotten his hands on the Cosmic Annihilator, a deadly weapon that had been created by Darkseid, one of Superman's most feared foes. His creation was so powerful that it could blow up an entire planet with ease.

Darkseid had planned to use the Cosmic Annihilator during his invasion of Earth, but a team of heroes led by Superman defeated him. Before Darkseid could use the weapon, he was sent back to Apokolips.

As Darkseid vanished, the Cosmic Annihilator fell from his hands and was lost somewhere in Gotham Harbor.

Until now. Now it was in the hands of Matches Malone. A homeless woman had found it a few nights back and sold it to him.

Matches smirked. *And I only had to pay her fifty bucks for it,* he thought.

Matches Malone couldn't even use such a big weapon all by himself. So he decided to sell it to the highest bidder.

Batman and Robin had been following him for several days and nights, waiting for Matches to meet with his buyer. That way, the Dynamic Duo would be able to capture them both — and retrieve the Cosmic Annihilator.

And now was the time to strike!

Robin turned off his motorcycle as he neared the pier and coasted the rest of the way in. He didn't want Matches to hear the roar of the engine and realize that he was being followed.

At the pier, Matches Malone looked around nervously. He didn't see his buyer anywhere.

From behind a crate, Robin watched Matches pace back and forth. Then he felt a hand on his shoulder. Robin whirled around to see Batman standing there. He had removed his old man disguise and was now wearing his super hero uniform.

Pointing to Matches Malone, Batman whispered, "The buyer should be here in a few more minutes. Once he arrives, we'll catch them both."

Just then, they heard a loud scream.

AHHHHHHHH!

Robin though it sounded like a scared child. "What do we do?" Robin asked. "If we leave to help, Matches Malone might get away!"

"It doesn't matter, Robin," Batman said. "Saving innocent lives is our top priority."

Batman and Robin raced toward the source of the scream. They saw an old apartment building on fire. Most of the people had escaped, but there were two children trapped on the seventh floor. They shouted for help from the windows, waving their arms frantically back and forth.

"Help! Help!" cried the young boy.

"Somebody save us!" the older girl shouted.

FWIP! Batman and Robin threw their Batropes to the top of the building. *CLANK! CLINK!* The hooks caught hold. With practiced ease, the two heroes quickly climbed up the ropes toward the children.

As they reached the third floor, Batman looked up. The kids were trapped on the seventh floor. The kids could see the heroes climbing up toward them now. Batman's uniform had been designed to frighten criminals. He certainly didn't want to scare these kids, though, so he made sure to greet them kindly.

"Hello," he called out to them. "I'm Batman and this is my partner, Robin. What are your names?"

"I'm Brooke," said the young girl. "And this is my little brother, Gus."

"It's nice to meet you, Brooke and Gus," Batman told them, still climbing. "We're going to get you out of there right away."

WHOOOOOOOOOSH! A large flame burst out from the windows on the third floor next to Batman and Robin. Soon, the flames would spread to the seventh floor.

"It's getting hotter!" Brooke cried.

"Help!" pleaded Gus.

"Batman," Robin said, "we may not get there soon enough to save them!"

"You're right," Batman said. "This calls for Plan B."

Batman braced himself against the building. "I know you're both scared, Brooke and Gus, but I need you to do something," he said. "I need you to jump out the window."

The two children looked at each other uncertainly. Gus hugged Brooke tightly.

"You're going to have to trust me," the Dark Knight called out. "My partner and I will catch you."

It was obvious that Brooke and Gus didn't want to jump out the window, but the fire had almost reached them. They had no choice.

Brooke carefully helped her little brother onto the windowsill. Then, carefully, his sister lowered him by his hands, and reluctantly dropped him. Robin leaned back on his rope and wrapped it around his waist tightly. A moment later, he caught Gus in his strong hands. To an outside observer, the feat looked impossible. But Robin had been trained to handle this kind of situation.

Robin had spent countless hours practicing acrobatics, martial arts, and gymnastics in the Batcave with the Dark Knight himself.

Robin zipped down his rope, landing softly on the street. He gently set Gus on the ground.

"Wow!" Gus cried out. "That was awesome! Can we do it again?!"

Robin smiled. "I think once is enough for tonight," he said.

"Your brother is safe," Batman told Brooke. "Now it's your turn."

Brooke hesitated. It was a long drop, but the fire was getting closer. She knew there was no choice, but that didn't make jumping any easier. "Are you sure that you're going to catch me?" she asked.

"Completely sure," Batman answered, holding out his hands.

"Okay, then," Brooke said. She climbed onto the sill and then leaped out the window. As she jumped, Brooke caught her foot on the sill and fell, off balance, to the side!

Batman saw that he was out of position to catch the falling girl. With the speed of an expert mountain climber, Batman pushed off the building with his feet and skittered across the wall toward Brooke. In one deft movement, Batman stopped his momentum directly beneath the young girl and caught her in his arms.

Batman and Robin quickly checked over both children to make sure they were okay. They then brought them back to their parents.

Moments later, they were racing to the pier. When they arrived, however, they were too late.

Matches Malone was gone!

"He must have already sold the Cosmic Annihilator," Robin said.

"It seems likely," Batman agreed. "But don't worry. We can still catch them."

The two heroes raced to the top of a nearby warehouse and looked around. They had a good view from up top. As Batman glanced across the horizon, he caught sight of Matches Malone walking back toward the subway station.

"There he is!" Robin said. "Get him!"

The two heroes climbed onto Robin's motorcycle. **VROOOOOOOOOOM!** They raced toward the criminal.

A minute later, the super heroes caught up with Matches Malone just as he was about to enter the subway. Batman leaped off the motorcycle as Robin screeched to a stop. Soaring through the air, Batman landed next to Matches Malone and knocked him to the pavement. The briefcase he was carrying hit the ground and burst open. Countless hundred-dollar bills spilled out.

Batman grabbed Matches by the collar of his suit. "Who bought the Cosmic Annihilator from you?" Batman asked.

Matches stiffened his upper lip. "He calls himself the Master of Ceremonies," he said. "But you'll never find him!"

"We'll see about that," Batman said. He searched through Matches' pockets for clues.

Batman found a small piece of paper that looked like a ticket. It read: ADMIT ONE TO THE FIRST ANNUAL SUPER-VILLAIN CONVENTION.

"That's where we'll find the Master of Ceremonies," Batman said. "And the Cosmic Annihilator."

Batman zip-tied Matches Malone's hands and called for a police officer to come and pick him up. A few moments later, Matches Malone was headed to the Gotham City jail, and the Dynamic Duo was headed back to the Batcave.

* * *

Later, Robin was sitting in the Batcave eating lunch. As he ate, the Boy Wonder told their butler, Alfred Pennyworth, everything that had happened that night.

"If Batman and I go to that convention," Robin began, "we'll have to fight hundreds of superpowered criminals!" Robin let out a sigh. "We're good at crime fighting, but I don't know if even we can handle that many villains at once."

Batman's voice came from behind Robin. "Exactly," he said. "That's why Batman and Robin won't be attending the First Annual Super-Villain Crime Convention."

"We won't?" Robin said, turning to look at his mentor. However, Batman was standing in the shadows of the Batcave and Robin couldn't see him clearly.

"No," Batman answered. He took two steps into the light. He looked exactly like Matches Malone! He was wearing the same green plaid suit.

Batman also wore the same tinted glasses. He'd even practiced making awkward small talk in a nasal voice, just like the real Matches Malone.

"Batman and Robin won't be there," Batman said with a grin. "But Matches Malone will be."

CHAPTER 2

SUPER-VILLAIN CONVENTION

The following day, Batman arrived at a secret convention center disguised as Matches Malone. His costume consisted of his regular plaid outfit, tinted glasses, and a prosthetic nose and chin attached with special glue that only he knew how to remove. To anyone else, these prosthetics looked just like the real thing.

At the door to the convention center, a tall man in a black tuxedo greeted him. The man wore a domino mask that hid his true identity.

As he shook Batman's hand, the man smiled warmly. "Matches Malone," he said, "I am so very pleased that you decided to accept my invitation."

Batman realized that this must be the Master of Ceremonies. "I wouldn't have missed it for anything," he said in a flat and nasally voice that was identical to the voice of the real Matches Malone. "So, how's the weather treatin' ya?"

The Master of Ceremonies rolled his eyes, then left Batman to greet another pair of criminals who had just arrived.

It seems I have the annoying small talk down, Batman thought.

As Batman entered the main lobby, he couldn't believe what he saw. Everywhere he looked, there were super-villains.

A large group of criminals were gathered around the buffet table, acting just like normal folks would. They were eating nachos and pizza, and sipping drinks while chatting with each other. On the other side of the lobby, the main schedule was written on a large board. Batman walked over.

There were several panel speakers scheduled for the day. Gorilla Grodd, Monsieur Mallah, and Titano were hosting a panel later that afternoon titled "On Being an Ape." Next to the title, there was a small blurb that read: "Being a gorilla in a world full of Homo sapiens can be a real challenge. Gorilla Grodd shares his helpful tips for apes considering a career in crime!"

Batman grabbed a flyer and stuffed it in his pocket. *Robin will get a kick out of this,* he thought.

Beneath that was a panel discussion titled "How to Improve your Super-Villain Hideout." Beneath, it read, "Just because you're a villain, doesn't mean you need to be a slob!"

Below that Batman read about another seminar, "Choosing your Super-Villain Name!" The description read, "What's in a name? Our panel of experts will discuss the importance of choosing a super-villain name that reflects both who you are and who you hope someday to be!"

Batman saw that later in the day there would be an award ceremony. The Joker and Lex Luthor were going to be officially inducted into the Super-Villain Hall of Fame. There were two life-size cardboard cutouts of the villains standing beside the announcement.

At the bottom of the cutouts someone —
Batman thought he recognized the Joker's
handwriting — had written "The Brave and
the Bald!"

The Dark Knight had hidden a small
microphone in the collar of his plaid
suit, and a listening device in his ear let
him communicate with Robin. Looking
around the main hall, Batman whispered,
"Robin, I wish you could see all this. It's
unbelievable!"

Back in the Batcave, Robin was using
the Batcomputer to look up the convention
center's blueprints. They could possibly
help Robin figure out where the Cosmic
Annihilator was hidden.

Batman entered the main convention
hall, observing everything around him.

Hanging from the ceiling was the spaceship used by Superman's old enemy, Brainiac. Before Superman captured him, Brainiac had used his ship to travel through outer space, shrinking cities and placing them inside bottles. Now, the ship was simply a decoration.

All the same, the ship made Batman shiver.

Batman continued walking. Near the entrance to the main hall was a small table with a sign that read, "Free Clown Faces!"

Seated behind the table was the Joker! He was calling out to people as they walked by, "Stop by and I'll give you a free clown face! Free clown faces for everyone!"

"Bring the kiddies!" Joker called out. *HAHAHAHAHAHA!*

Only one person was waiting to receive a free clown face, and she wasn't a kid. Harley Quinn, Joker's main squeeze and partner in crime, was jumping up and down on a pogo stick with one hand raised in the air.

"Ooh! Me! Me!" Harley shouted. "I want a clown face! I'm next in line! Me! Me! Pick me!"

The Joker was clearly trying to ignore her. But every now and then, he would turn around and snarl, "Cut it out, Harley! You're scaring off the customers!"

No one else wanted to get a free clown face. Not even other villains trusted the Joker to put anything on their faces.

"Matches, my friend," Joker called after spotting Batman disguised as Matches.

"Come get a free clown face, Matches!" Joker said. "After all, everyone loves a clown! HAHAHA!"

"That ain't fair!" Harley complained. "I've been waiting here for hours! When's it gonna be my turn?"

The Joker leaned over to Batman. "Ignore her, Matches," he said. "Just pretend she isn't even there."

"Maybe later, Joker," the Dark Knight said. Then he quickly turned around and headed in a different direction.

"My disguise must be working," Batman whispered to Robin. "Even the Joker didn't notice I'm not the real Matches Malone."

Hanging from the ceiling of the main hall was a large banner advertising the upcoming auction.

The banner promised that all proceeds from the auction would go to the Super-Villain Legal Defense Fund. It listed several items that would be sold at the auction:

The Colonel of Crime's Crimi-Tank

A Replica of Two-Face's Special Coin

Boss Haney's Colossal Typewriter

The Ultimate Death Trap

Batman was familiar with nearly all of those items. He still remembered the time that the Colonel of Crime had driven his Crimi-Tank through Gotham City. The Crimi-Tank was a cross between an armored truck and a tank, armed with dozens of weapons, including a giant steam shovel, a mechanical arm, and two giant buzz saws that could chop down anything that got in their way.

Batman was also familiar with Two-Face's contribution to the auction. In fact, the Dynamic Duo had once been tied to one side of that giant silver dollar and nearly tossed into the ocean!

Batman had never seen the Ultimate Death Trap, but he'd certainly heard of it. The Death Trap had been created by a great magician who had intended to use it in one of his escape acts. After it was built, the magician realized that there was no way to escape from the device. He hid the Death Trap so that it could never be used. Apparently, however, someone had found it. Batman shuddered at the thought of it falling into the hands of the Joker or the Riddler.

But right there, listed as the very last item for sale at the auction . . .

. . . was the Cosmic Annihilator!

"Robin," Batman whispered into his microphone. "It looks like they're planning to auction off the Cosmic Annihilator later today. That means it's probably being held with all the other auction items. See if you can find a very large storage room somewhere in the building."

Robin zoomed through the convention center blueprints on the Batcave computer. "There's a storage space branching off from the east side of the convention center," he reported. "That might be the right place."

"Good work," Batman said. "I'm heading there now."

Just then, the Master of Ceremonies approached Batman. "Matches, my friend! I've been looking all over for you!"

"Yeah?" Batman said, immediately switching back to the flat, nasally voice of Matches Malone. "What do you want?"

"There's something I'd like to show you," he said.

"Well, I'm kind of busy at the moment," Batman whined.

"It will just take a minute, I promise," the strange man said. "And I think you'll find it worth your while."

The Dark Knight did not want to go anywhere with the Master of Ceremonies, but if he refused to accompany him, it might look suspicious. "Okay," Batman finally said. "But just for a minute."

Batman followed the Master of Ceremonies out of the main hall. He led him into a small storage room.

Once they were inside, the Master of Ceremonies pulled out a deadly energy blaster!

"What's the big idea?" Batman asked, still pretending to be Matches Malone. "Is this your idea of a joke?"

"Not at all," the Master of Ceremonies said. He raised his arm and aimed the energy blaster at Batman! "I don't know who you really are, but you're definitely not Matches Malone!"

"What are you talking about?" Batman cried out. He was surprised. How could the Master of Ceremonies have figured out the truth?

"You look just like him, I admit," the strange man said. "But you made one big mistake, my friend."

"And what's that?" Batman asked.

"The real Matches Malone would have struck up unsufferable and annoying conversations with several guests by now," he said. "And you haven't talked to anybody but me!"

He was right! Batman had been too busy surveying the scene to make small talk with the other villains at the convention.

"Now start barking, and tell me who you really are," the Master of Ceremonies ordered. "Or I'll show you my bite!"

CHAPTER 3

A HEATED ARGUMENT

Batman had to think fast. He couldn't let the Master of Ceremonies figure out who he really was, but he couldn't let the man shoot him, either.

Batman held his hands up. "Whoa there, buddy!" he said. "It's really me! It's Matches Malone!"

"Then how do you explain your behavior at the convention?" asked the Master of Ceremonies.

"After I sold you the Cosmic Annihilator last night," Batman explained, "I went out and used that briefcase full of money and bought all kinds of cool stuff!"

The Master of Ceremonies tilted his head. Batman could tell the villain was skeptical.

"I'm exhausted," Batman continued. "I just don't have the energy today to talk all that much!"

Batman did his best to look tired. However, he could see that the Master of Ceremonies still wasn't convinced.

"Look," said Batman. "I can prove it to you." Batman began to dig through his pockets. "It's here somewhere," he muttered. "I know I kept that parking ticket!"

"Parking ticket?" asked the Master of Ceremonies.

"Yep," Batman said. "I got a parking ticket outside the mall I visited in downtown Gotham. It listed the time as 12:15 in the a.m.! That will prove I was out late."

Batman produced a slip of paper he'd gotten from a booth earlier. "Here it is," he said, holding it out.

When the Master of Ceremonies lifted his hand to take the ticket, Batman used that moment to leap forward and hit the masked villain as hard as he could.

THUDDD! The Master of Ceremonies fell to the floor, unconscious.

"That was a close one!" Robin's voice came from the earpiece.

"Yes," Batman agreed. "If he saw through my disguise, then it's only a matter of time until someone else does, too. I need to find the Cosmic Annihilator and get out of here as quickly as possible."

The Dark Knight tied up the Master of Ceremonies, then headed back toward the east side of the building. On the way, he passed one room where his old enemy, Catwoman, was giving a seminar on how to open locked objects.

As he walked by, Batman heard her say, "Any fool can blow up a safe with explosives. But being a thief is about more than just stealing things. It's about stealing . . . with style!"

In the next room, the Mad Mod, the fashion-forward enemy of the Teen Titans, was teaching criminals to dress for success.

"If you dress like a two-bit thug," the Mad Mod said, "then that's how others will perceive you. But you are not a two-bit thug. You're a super-villain. So, you need to wear a costume that says 'I've got superpowers, I'm evil, and I feel good about who I am!'" The entire room burst into cheers.

Apparently even super-villains need support groups, thought Batman.

But Batman was starting to think that maybe a Super-Villain Crime Convention wasn't such a bad idea. He knew that many villains were unable to see the good in themselves, and so they behaved like criminals.

Or they're just dark, evil people, Batman thought.

Lost in thought, Batman walked right into a crowd of super-villains who seemed to be arguing about something. Batman wanted to avoid this situation, but it was too late. The Penguin grabbed him by the collar and pulled him into the middle of the small crowd.

"Matches," said the Penguin, "maybe you can help resolve an argument we're having."

"Sure," Batman replied. "What's it about?"

The Penguin pointed to several super-villains. Batman immediately recognized them. They were the archenemies of his friend, the Flash! One was Heatwave, whose flamethrower could burn through almost anything.

Standing next to Heatwave was Captain Cold, who had a Cold-Gun that could freeze people into solid ice. Next there was the Mirror Master, who was able to step inside one mirror and come out another anywhere in the world. Standing beside them was Captain Boomerang, whose boomerangs exploded like bombs and could cut through solid steel.

These were dangerous men even under the best of circumstances.

"These costumed clowns think that their archenemy, the Flash, is a greater challenge than my old foe, Batman!" the Penguin said, gesturing at the men beside him.

Next to the Penguin were several of Batman's greatest enemies. There was Two-Face, who made life or death decisions with the flip of a coin.

Standing off to the side was Poison Ivy, who loved plants but hated people. Standing next to him was the Riddler, who enjoyed solving puzzles almost as much as he enjoyed stealing money. Finally, there was the Joker, Batman's most dangerous enemy.

"Batman isn't so tough!" shouted Captain Cold. "He doesn't have any superpowers at all. He's just some normal guy in black pajamas!" Captain Cold pointed up one finger on each side of his head, making bat ears. "Oooh! Scary!"

Two-Face shoved Captain Cold. "Batman is *twice* the super hero that the Flash is!" he shouted.

Captain Cold pushed Two-Face back. "The Flash could run circles around Batman!"

So much for making friends, Batman thought.

A big fight was about to break out. Batman did not want to be in the middle of that. He needed to get out of there and find the Cosmic Annihilator before the auction began.

Just as the two groups of villains were about to start fighting, a low, calm voice called out. "Actually," it said, "neither the Flash nor Batman are very impressive."

Everyone stopped shouting and turned around to look. It was Superman's archenemy, Lex Luthor. "The Flash has one superpower," Luthor continued. "Just one. And Batman? He's a decent detective, I suppose, but he has no superpowers at all. Now imagine if your enemy had multiple superpowers."

Batman could see that the other villains were afraid of Lex Luthor. No one dared to interrupt him, and everyone kept a safe distance as he slowly sauntered over to the scene.

"Yes, the Flash has super-speed, It's true," Luthor said. "But Superman has super-speed as well as super-strength! Plus he can fly. And he has heat vision!"

"That's four superpowers," the Calculator observed. "So far."

"Don't forget his X-ray vision that lets him see through almost anything," Luthor said. "But worst of all? He's invulnerable!"

"What does that mean?" asked Heatwave.

"It means that nothing can hurt him, you idiot," Luthor explained.

"Bullets bounce right off his chest," Luthor added. "Lightning just tickles him."

"Four superpowers plus two superpowers," said the Calculator. "According to my calculations, that equals six superpowers in total!"

The Penguin shoved Calculator out of the way. "Look, Luthor," he said, "no one is arguing that Superman isn't tough. But Batman . . ."

"Batman? Batman?!" Luthor said. He began to laugh. "Well, I suppose if I were you, Penguin, then maybe I would be impressed by the Batman. I mean, you're not exactly a master criminal, are you? You use umbrellas to commit crimes and you waddle around like an overstuffed bird! Batman might pose a serious threat to you and your lunatic friends. But not to me."

The other villains were starting to get angry. They were afraid of Lex Luthor, but they weren't going to let him stand there and insult them.

Two-Face stepped forward. "You think Superman is the best?" he said with a sneer. "Well, I've got one word for you: Kryptonite."

HAHAHAHAA! The other villains started to laugh at Luthor.

"Oooh, Superman is so powerful!" the Joker taunted. "He's got so many powers! There's no way that you could possibly defeat him! HAHAHA! Unless, of course, you're holding a silly green rock!"

"Stop laughing!" Luthor shouted. "Yes, he has a vulnerability to green Kryptonite, but—"

The Joker laughed even harder. "Oh, poor Luthor! You say you're a genius, but you aren't even smart enough to carry some Kryptonite with you!"

Lex Luthor pushed the Joker. **THUMPP!** The laughing clown stumbled backward, collided into the Calculator, and then fell onto the Penguin. With that, a huge fight broke out! All the villains started attacking each other. As the super-villains traded punches and kicks, Batman quietly tried to sneak away. So far, no one had noticed. Just a few more steps and he'd be clear of the squabbling super-villains!

But, just then, he heard a terrible noise. **ZAPPPP!**

Heatwave had pulled out his flamethrower and fired a blast. At the last second, someone had bumped into him.

The blast missed its original target. Instead, it hit one of the metal cables that were holding up Brainiac's spaceship that was hanging from the ceiling. The cable melted and snapped. **SNAP!** The ship fell toward the ground.

It was going to land on the Penguin. It would kill him. Batman couldn't let that happen! The Penguin was a criminal, but Batman protected all lives, even the lives of villains.

Batman leaped forward and shoved the Penguin, knocking him out of the way of the falling spaceship.

WHAM! The spaceship crashed to the floor.

All the super-villains stopped their fighting.

Silently, they all stared at the man who looked like Matches Malone, but moved like a trained athlete.

"Something funny's going on here," the Joker said. "Since when does Matches move like that?"

"Have you been working out, Matches?" Heatwave asked.

"Riddle me this," added the Riddler, "it looks like Matches Malone and it sounds like Matches Malone, but it jumps like a rabbit and it rescues penguins. What could it be?"

A voice called out, "I think I may know the answer to that riddle."

Batman looked up and saw that the man speaking was the Master of Ceremonies!

He must have somehow untied himself, Batman thought.

"Unless I miss my guess," said the Master of Ceremonies, "we just caught ourselves a Batman!"

CHAPTER 4

TOO MANY VILLAINS

The Penguin waddled back to his feet. Batman had managed to save him, but now he was in serious trouble.

"What's happening, Batman?" Robin's voice whispered into Batman's earpiece. "Are you okay?"

The Dark Knight took a few steps back from the costumed criminals. He whispered into the hidden microphone, "Robin, I think I may need to make a hasty retreat. How do I get from the main hall to the storage area as quickly as possible?"

"Don't run away, Batman," the Joker said between chuckles. "We just want to play!"

Batman was not a coward, but he also wasn't a fool. He knew that his chance of defeating that many super-villains at once was slim. It was time to go.

The super hero raced away from the crowd of villains. They immediately began chasing him. As Batman ran, Robin called out directions to him.

"Head toward the eastern corridor," Robin said. "Once you get there, you'll need to take the elevator down to the basement level."

As Batman neared the elevator, he pulled out an exploding Batarang and threw it at the elevator doors. *BOOOOOM!!*

The doors blew off their hinges. The hero could see the metal cable that pulled the elevator car up and down. Without a moment's hesitation, Batman leaped into the elevator shaft and began climbing down the metal cable. As he did, he removed his Matches Malone disguise.

"Come back!" he heard the Joker call out. "We aren't done with you yet, Batman!"

Batman quickly reached the lower level. He tried to pry the elevator doors open with his fingers, but it was no use. From above, he could hear the super-villains shoving each other out of the way as they all tried to grab the metal cable and slide down after him.

"Out of my way!" one voice called out.

"Move over!" cried another.

"Get off of my foot!" shouted a third.

Batman realized he had one big advantage: the super-villains were not good at working together. Even so, it was only a matter of time before they caught up with him.

Batman was finally able to pull the doors of the elevator open. He then jumped out of the elevator shaft. The Dark Knight looked around the storage area, trying to find the Cosmic Annihilator. He couldn't leave this crazy convention without it.

Batman climbed up on Two-Face's giant coin. Then he leaped off of it and landed on top of the highest stack of wooden crates. From there, he had a good view of the room.

Batman searched frantically for any sign of the Cosmic Annihilator. As he looked around the large room, Batman saw that several super-villains had already arrived. Standing near the open elevator doors were the Joker, Heatwave, Captain Cold, and Poison Ivy! And more costumed criminals were arriving with every second.

Batman finally caught a glimpse of the Cosmic Annihilator. "I've found it!" he told Robin. "Just a few more seconds, and I'll have it!"

However, Batman did not notice the old, cobwebbed mirror hanging from the wall. Just as Batman reached for the Cosmic Annihilator, a gloved fist came out from the mirror, hitting him right in the jaw. *KAPOW!*

Batman fell to the floor.

The Mirror Master climbed out from the mirror. "Did you forget about me, Batman?" Mirror Master asked.

Before Batman could get back up, Poison Ivy was by his side. **FWOOOOSH!** She blew a burst of toxin at him. Immediately he felt sleepy. "Do you like that, Batman?" she asked. "That's a perfume I made from the petals of a very rare flower known as the Sleeping Orchid. They say that one whiff is enough to put someone to sleep for hours!"

But Batman could barely hear what she was saying. *I must try to stay awake,* he thought. But his head felt so heavy, and the world seemed to be spinning. Batman's eyes closed.

The Master of Ceremonies stood above the fallen hero. "Nicely done, Poison Ivy!" he said. "What should we do with him?"

The Joker laughed. "Oh, I think I may have an idea or two," he said.

* * *

One hour later, Batman awoke. The first thing he noticed was that he couldn't move. And upon opening his eyes, he saw that he was upside down!

While he'd been sleeping, the villains had tied him up in chains and now he was hanging inside the Ultimate Death Trap. It was a large glass container with several small holes at the very bottom. Batman could see that water was slowly bubbling up from the small holes. Soon, the water would rise and fill the glass case — with him inside!

Standing around the Death Trap were all the super-villains from the convention.

The villains were watching him and grinning. The situation was dire. *At least they didn't notice my prosthetic chin and nose,* he thought. *If they had, they'd all have recognized me as Bruce Wayne!*

"It's so good of you to wake up," said the Master of Ceremonies. "We were worried that you were going to sleep through your own death!"

"You don't want to do this," Batman told the super-villains.

GURGLE! GURGLE! Water bubbled up from the bottom of the Death Trap, inching closer and closer to Bruce's face.

"Don't we? I think we do," the Master of Ceremonies said. He smiled cruelly. "I have to thank you, Batman. Your death will be the perfect way to end the First Annual Super-Villain Crime Convention!"

CHAPTER 5

DEATH TRAP

The Dark Knight knew that he had only a couple of minutes before the water would rise above his head and he would drown. He struggled to break free from the chains, but they were too tight. Batman had studied escapology for years, but he doubted that even Houdini would be able to free himself from this sticky situation.

From inside his ear, Batman could hear Robin's voice. "Batman, are you okay?" he asked. "What's happening?"

Batman thought carefully. He not only had to escape from an inescapable death trap, he would also have to confront the crowd of super-villains who were standing outside the Death Trap, and then grab the Cosmic Annihilator.

"Robin," Batman whispered into the microphone. "I need your help."

"Sure," Robin replied. "What is it?"

"I need you to shut off the power to this convention center for exactly ten seconds," Batman whispered. "Can you do that right now?"

"No problem," Robin told him. "I can use the Batcomputer to access the city's power grid."

"Thanks," Batman replied. "And please hurry!"

Robin quickly typed several commands into the Batcomputer. Within a few seconds, he had gained access to the entire city's power grid.

"Okay," Robin told Batman. "In three seconds, all the power will be shut off, including the building you're in."

Batman counted down in his head. A moment later, the power went out in the convention center. The lights turned off with a **CLICK!** With the power out, the Death Trap restraints snapped open. Without making a single sound, Batman squirmed out of the container.

"Hey, is this some kind of joke?" the Joker called out.

"Who turned out the lights?" cried Two-Face.

The dark was something most people tried to avoid. However, Batman was right at home in the shadows. On his hands and knees, he silently scurried toward where he'd heard the Penguin's voice. Batman placed himself between the Death Trap and the Penguin.

WHUMP! He kicked at the Penguin's legs, knocking him onto his back.

"**OW!**" the Penguin cried.

Batman stood, and yelled, "Take that, Penguin!" Just as quickly, he dropped to his knees and scurried away.

Heatwave and Captain Cold couldn't see anything inside the dark room, but they aimed their guns at where the voice was coming from. Then they both pulled their triggers.

FWOOOOM! Blazing heat and freezing cold hit the glass walls of the Death Trap at the exact same moment. The thick glass cracked and then shattered into a million pieces with a loud *CRASSSSH!*

"What was that?" Joker asked.

"It didn't sound good!" cried Riddler.

"I don't like our odds of survival," shouted Calculator. "It's time to leave!"

Batman figured the villains would get scared more easily in the dark. He was glad to hear their panicked voices.

At that moment, the lights came back on. The villains were stunned to see that the Death Trap was destroyed . . . and Batman was gone!

RUMMMMMMBLE! The sound of a powerful engine's revving filled the room.

Batman had climbed inside the Crimi-Tank!

Captain Cold shot his Cold-Gun. *ZAP!*

Heatwave fired his Flamethrower. *KIRRRRRSH!*

Captain Boomerang threw his explosive boomerangs. *BANG! POW!*

The Penguin sprayed acid from his acid-tipped umbrella. *HISSSSSSSSSSS!*

All the different super-villains used every weapon they had at their disposal to try to stop the Crimi-Tank.

However, the Colonel of Crime had built the Crimi-Tank to survive pretty much anything. All the ice, flames, acid, bullets, and explosions bounced harmlessly off the Crimi-Tank as Batman drove it toward the crowd of super-villains.

Batman activated the steam shovel and used it to scoop up all the villains in one swipe.

THUMP! Batman dumped them into a giant, wooden crate.

Once they were all inside, Batman used the Crimi-Tank's mechanical arm to close the lid on the crate.

Now no one would be able to escape.

When all the super-villains had been captured, Batman climbed outside the Crimi-Tank and picked up the Cosmic Annihilator.

"Batman, are you okay?" Robin asked.

"I'm fine," Batman said. "Thanks to you, that is."

"No problem!" Robin answered proudly.

Batman carefully placed the Cosmic Annihilator in another crate, relieved it had not fallen into a villain's hands.

"Please call the police and give them this address," Batman told Robin. He glanced at the crate filled with super-villains. "And tell them to bring plenty of handcuffs," he added.

Batman could hear Robin's laughter through his earpiece. "It sounds like you've had a really busy day!" Robin said.

Batman smirked. "Well," he said, "I suppose you could say it was an *unconventional* one."

From inside the giant wooden crate, a loud groan came out. "That isn't funny, Batman!" the Joker yelled. "And you say my jokes are bad!"

But Batman couldn't hear the Joker. He was already climbing back up through the convention center's elevator shaft with the Cosmic Annihilator in tow.

THE DARK KNIGHT

REAL NAME:
Bruce Wayne

OCCUPATION:
Businessman by day,
crime fighter by night

BASE:
Gotham City

HEIGHT:
6 feet, 2 inches

WEIGHT:
210 pounds

EYES:
Blue

HAIR:
Black

As a young child, Bruce Wayne saw his parents murdered in cold blood. He soon swore an oath to rid Gotham of its criminal element, and to keep the city safe. To achieve this goal, he trained in crime-fighting skills, including criminology, detective skills, martial arts, gymnastics, disguise, and escape artistry. Donning a costume inspired by his fearful run-in with bats at a young age, the Dark Knight aims to strike the same fear into his opponents.

- The Dark Knight is one of the most intelligent people alive, and also one of the greatest fighters.

- He depends on Alfred Pennyworth, his lifelong friend and butler, as both Batman and Bruce Wayne.

- The Dark Knight despises firearms and refuses to use them, and is opposed to the taking of human life.

- Batman has trained many crime fighters, including several Robins, Batgirl, Batwoman, and others.

BIOGRAPHIES

PAUL WEISSBURG lives with his wife, Mie, in Rock Island, Illinois, where he teaches political science at Augustana College. Paul read his first comic book in the summer of 1976 and has been an avid comic book reader and writer ever since.

LUCIANO VECCHIO was born in 1982 and currently lives in Buenos Aires, Argentina. With experience in illustration, animation, and comics, his works have been published in the US, Spain, UK, France, and Argentina. Credits include *Ben 10* (DC Comics), *Cruel Thing* (Norma), *Unseen Tribe* (Zuda Comics), and *Sentinels* (Drumfish Productions).

GLOSSARY

awkward (AWK-wurd)—not able to relax and talk to people easily, or diffcult and embarrassing

brooding (BROOD-ing)—kept worrying, thinking, or being angry about something

convention (kuhn-VEN-shuhn)—a large gathering of people who have the same interests

dolt (DOHLT)—a dumb or stupid person

nasal (NAY-zuhl)—spoken through the nose rather than the mouth, or having to do with your nose

pier (PEER)—a platform that extends over a body of water

plaid (PLAD)—a pattern of squares in cloth formed by weaving stripes of different widths and colors that cross each other

prey (PRAY)—an animal that is hunted by another animal for food, or the victim of an attack or robbery

prosthetic (pross-THET-ik)—an artificial device that replaces a missing part of a body

unconventional (un-kuhn-VEN-shuhn-uhl)—not traditional or normal

DISCUSSION QUESTIONS

1. Which super-villain in this story do you think would be the most dangerous for Batman to face alone? Discuss your answers.

2. There are many kinds of conventions, like comic book conventions and business conventions. If you could create any kind of convention, what kind would you choose?

3. This book has ten illustrations. Which one is your favorite? Why?

WRITING PROMPTS

1. Batman's known as the World's Greatest Detective because he has sharp senses and an attentive, clever mind. Write a short story about Batman where he uses his detective skills to solve a crime.

2. In this story, Batman goes undercover to catch the bad guys. Write another story about Batman where he uses his physical abilities and gadgets to defeat a group of villains.

3. In this story, Batman is outnumbered by his enemies. Write about a time when you were outnumbered. What happened? How did you feel?

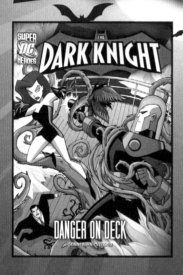

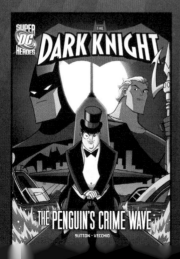